Jade's Life Skills Series

Learning Something New

Or

Sail to the Ocean!

By Asaf Shani

Illustrated by
Louise Gale Budol

Dad and Jade picked Andy up from kindergarten. In the car, Dad turned to Andy and Jade, who were buckled in their safety seats, and said, "Today, I have a surprise for you." "Surprise, surprise!" Andy shouted, clapping his hands. "What is the surprise?" Jade asked hopefully. Dad said, "We're going to a horse ranch!" "Horse ranch?" Jade asked. "Yes," Dad answered. "Where the two of you can pat and even ride a horse." "Yippee!" Andy and Jade said together. "Horse ranch, horse ranch!" they called while Dad started the engine.

Soon, Jade and Andy saw fewer and fewer houses. Instead they saw wide fields and many trees. "The horse farm," Dad said "is just outside our city. We're almost there." A few minutes later, Dad parked outside a high brown fence with an open gate. As everyone climbed out of the car, a girl came through the gate leading a big brown horse. She wore a strange helmet, tight grey trousers, and high black boots. The horse looked at them and neighed. Jade felt very excited.

Dad put Andy in the baby carrier and held Jade's hand as they walked through the gate. Hay was scattered on the ground. The strange smell reminded Jade of the zoo. To their left were the stables, and in the different boxes were all kinds of horses: big brown horses, white thinner ones, and even a few really small ones. Dad pointed at the little ones and said, "These are ponies. They won't grow any bigger." "Can we pat them?" Jade asked, excited. "Sure!" Dad answered. "And also ride one!"

A young girl approached. "Hi Danielle," Dad said. "Hey!" said the girl, with a big smile. "Meet Jade and Andy," Dad said, and Danielle said, "Hi! Andy and Jade, would you like to come with me into the stables?" "Yes please," Jade said. Danielle took Jade's hand and they all went inside. "I'm a riding instructor," said Danielle. "I teach children how to ride." Jade felt nervous so she let go of Danielle's hand and clung to Dad's leg. Andy clapped in his baby carrier. "This is Rainbow," Danielle said, pointing at a gray pony. Jade and Rainbow looked at each other. Although Rainbow wasn't much higher than Jade, she was afraid of him so she gripped Dad's leg tighter. Danielle smiled and patted Rainbow's back. "It's okay to feel afraid," Dad said softly to Jade while gently stroking her hair. "It's the first time you're so close to a horse."

"Watch," said Danielle. She picked up a strange brush that looked a bit like a shoe, placed it on her hand, and started brushing Rainbow's back. The pony lowered his head and gave a slight neigh as if saying 'I like that! Please continue!' "Animals talk," Danielle said. "What?" Jade asked. "I've never heard an animal talk." Danielle said, "They have their own language that is different than the language we speak. You can learn to understand their sounds and gestures, and understand what they are 'saying'." Jade looked at Rainbow who was eating hay and didn't seem to be saying anything.

5

"Horses, for example," said Danielle, "speak also with their ears. If a horse lays his ears back, it means he's upset. If he pricks up his ears, and swivels them towards whatever has caught his attention, he's interested." Jade thought that it would be nice if kids could speak with their ears too ... Danielle said to Jade, "Come, and brush Rainbow's back." Without taking her eyes off Rainbow's ears, Jade slowly approached. Danielle put the brush on Jade's hand and guided it along Rainbow's back. She showed Jade how to lay an apple on her open palm so Rainbow wouldn't bite her by accident while biting on the apple. Jade was sure Rainbow was smiling at her.

Slowly, slowly, Jade felt more comfortable around Rainbow. She didn't feel nervous any longer and she even made braids in his mane. When Danielle offered Jade a ride on the pony, Jade immediately agreed. Danielle handed Jade a helmet and said, "We always wear helmets when we ride." When Danielle fastened it on Jade's head, Andy knocked on it and laughed. Danielle helped Jade mount Rainbow. Jade held the reins tight; her whole body was tense and alert. But after a few minutes walking around the arena while Danielle held the reins, and Dad watched close by, Jade started relaxing.

When Dad said it was time to go, Jade was very disappointed. Dad promised to come again soon. "Maybe you could take riding lessons," he said. "Really?" Jade asked. "Yippee!" They bid farewell to Danielle and Rainbow, and got into the car. "Where are we going?" Jade asked. "I don't recognize the way." Dad smiled cheekily. "Ummm ... we're going to another new place ..."

After driving for a while, Dad parked the car near funny wooden houses that Jade and Andy had never seen before. When Dad helped Jade and Andy out of the car, they clung to his legs in fear. Dad smiled, hugged them both, and said, "What you feel right now is what we feel when we are confronted with something new." Jade and Andy stared around. The wooden houses looked strange; the streets were made of little stones, and the smell was unusual. "New things will always look strange or funny or scary because they are new," Dad said. "I want to go home," Andy said. Dad said, "I'm here to keep you both safe. I'll be close and make sure you'll have fun." Andy nodded and Dad placed him in the baby carrier. "OK with you to walk around here?" Dad asked Jade. She nodded and Dad smiled, holding her hand tightly, and said, "Atta girl!"

As they walked along the strange street, Dad said, "This is a very old town. People lived here many, many years ago." "How old?" Jade asked. "Is this town older than you?" Dad laughed. "It's much older than me; in fact, it's older than the dad of Grandpa ...." Andy and Jade looked around in astonishment as they'd never seen anything so old. "Were dinosaurs living here?" Jade asked. Dad laughed again. "No, my love, the dinosaurs lived even before there were people." "Look!" Jade said. "Ice cream shop!" "Well, fancy that ..." Dad said with a slight smile.

"This ice cream shop is modern," Dad explained. When they entered, they saw buckets of ice cream in strange flavors like avocado, ginger, and basil. "It's important to try new things," Dad said, "although we have the urge to stick to what we know. So, who would like to try the avocado ice cream?" Andy turned his head away.

Jade said, "I'll try!" Dad smiled and the saleslady gave her a spoon with avocado ice cream. "Yuck!" Jade said. "It tastes like ... avocado ... I don't like it ..." Dad and Andy laughed. "That's perfectly okay you don't like it. The important thing is that you've tried!" The saleslady handed Jade a spoon with pistachio ice cream. Jade looked at it suspiciously and put it in her mouth. "Yummy!" Jade said. "I like it!" So, they bought double chocolate ice cream for Andy, marshmallow & pistachio for Jade, and vanilla & pistachio for Dad.

Later that evening, after Jade and Andy showered and brushed their teeth, the three sat on Jade's bed, planning to read a book. "So," Dad asked, "how was your day?" "Great!" Andy and Jade said together. "You've learnt quite a few new things today," Dad added. Andy nodded and Jade started counting aloud all the new things. "I brushed and rode a pony, I saw a very old town with strange buildings and roads, and finally tasted two new flavors of ice cream." Dad smiled. "Indeed, you sure got out of your comfort zone today." "Comfort what?" Jade asked.

"Comfort zone," Dad answered. "It's the collection of things we are used to doing, that we feel comfortable with. Imagine a place in your head that contains all the things you are used to doing—places you are familiar with, people you know, food that you are used to eating—all the things you already know." Jade imagined all the things Dad mentioned. "Comfort doesn't mean we love the things in our comfort zone. It means we are used to them." Jade listened. Andy played with Barnie. Dad continued, "Now, in order to learn something new, we must leave our comfort zone. Going outside it will always feel strange—we may feel fear, embarrassment, shame, or even feel stupid."

Jade imagined herself going out of her comfort zone. Dad continued, "Think how you felt around Rainbow today." He turned to Andy and said to him, "Do you remember you were afraid when we got to the old village?" Andy nodded and said, "I didn't like it." Dad smiled and touched the tip of Andy's nose. "This is how experiencing something new might feel. We have the urge to escape back to the familiar. But if we do, we'll never learn new things."

Comfort Zone

"Think what would have happened if you didn't have the courage to go close to Rainbow." Jade replied, "I would have missed such an amazing time." "Indeed!" Dad said. "Learning new things will always feel strange at the beginning. Learning new things means that you can accept that feeling, and do something new anyway, In order to learn something new, we must go out of our comfort zone into the feeling of 'not knowing'. That feeling might make us feel scared or even stupid." Jade sat silent and Dad continued, "You were brave to try new things today—you've touched the rainbow." He winked at her. "If you'll continue to try new things—to go outside your comfort zone—you'll reach the rainbow!"

"Today I'll tell you the story called Disco Braves the Open Ocean."
Dad opened the book and started reading. "A school of fish lived in a
beautiful lagoon. The water was crystal clear, the soft white sand was
dotted with beautiful corals and, although nothing really happened in
the lagoon, all the fish were happy. All but one. Little Disco was a
beautiful discus fish who found life in the lagoon too boring. He used
to say, 'Nothing really happens here. I feel that I'm turning into a
jelly fish from not doing anything ...' One day, Disco decided he'd had
enough and he started swimming outside of the lagoon. 'Don't go
there,' shouted the other fish. 'It's dangerous out there!' But Disco
didn't pay attention and continued to swim into the open ocean.

After a few hours, Disco became tired and hungry. How happy he was to see a juicy little worm floating in the water. He swam towards the worm. 'I wouldn't do that if I were you,' said a voice. Disco stopped and looked around. 'Who's speaking?' he asked. A purple octopus appeared from behind a rock. He swam towards Disco while putting one of his legs on his lips, signaling to Disco to be quiet. When the octopus got close, he stretched out another leg and pulled a transparent string that the worm was connected to. Disco hadn't noticed this string. As soon as the octopus pulled the string, the worm was yanked out of the water. Disco looked at the disappearing worm with astonishment. The octopus signaled and they dived deeper.

'Hi,' the octopus said, 'I'm Ronny.' 'I'm Disco... thank you for saving me from ... that thing ...' The octopus laughed. 'Look,' he said to Disco while pointing up to a rectangular object floating above. 'That's a fisherman's boat and they use worms as bait to catch creatures like us.' Disco heard a roaring sound as the propeller started circling, creating swirling currents. 'And this,' said the octopus with a smile, 'is the sound they make. When you see a floating worm, look for the object in the water above and, if you hear the roaring sound, you'll know that danger is coming.' Disco waved his fins in silence. He felt excited as he suddenly realized how much he had to learn about the great ocean.

'Can you teach me more?' asked Disco. Ronny laughed. 'Sure!' he said. 'First, let's eat something as I guess you are very hungry.' Disco nodded and Ronny pulled out a bunch of delicious seaweed hidden behind a coral. Ronny took Disco to a place where nets and broken floats lay on the seabed, explaining about the danger of each one. As the sun set, Ronny took Disco to his cave that was lighted by strange glowing fish. 'Hi guys,' said Ronny.

'Don't let all the things you've seen today frighten you,' said the octopus after they had their dinner. 'When I was small, and that was many, many years ago, I swam near a boat. A grandfather and his grandson were sitting there. The grandfather told the boy a sentence I've remembered ever since.' Ronny paused then continued, 'A ship in harbor is safe, but that is not what ships are made for.' Disco floated in silence, understanding the importance of this lesson. He said, 'I'm not a boat, but the lesson is clear: in order to live a full life, I have to swim into the unknown sea.' They floated in silence until the octopus said, 'Come; I'll show you where you can sleep.'

Disco spent a few more days with Ronny who taught him many things about sharks, whales, currents, storms, and the land above the sea. They ate together and swam in places Disco had never seen before. Although Disco was excited by all the new things, he started missing his friends in the lagoon. The next morning, he hugged his new friend goodbye. 'Until next time,' said the octopus and gave him a small bag of seaweed. 'Thank you,' said Disco with a smile, and started swimming towards the lagoon.

All the fish were very happy and excited to see Disco. He shared with them all the things he'd seen and learnt. A few days later, when the fish were swimming lazily in the calm lagoon, a muffled roaring sound was heard. Disco stopped immediately. 'What's wrong?' asked Berny, the maroon clownfish, but Disco didn't answer. Instead, he looked up to the sea's surface. A rectangle appeared along with a propeller which created small currents. Disco said, 'Guys, come with me now! We are all in danger!' He darted away from the floating boat towards the corals. All the fish followed. Soon after, a stick with a net at its end appeared in the water. It missed Berny, who was the last to enter the safety of the corals, by an inch. 'Thank you!' all the fish said to Disco. 'You've saved us!' Disco humbly smiled and felt his heart overflow with joy."

Dad closed the book and looked at Jade and Andy. "Life is like the ocean; we are meant to explore it!" He smiled and kissed Jade good night. He carried Andy to his bed and left the room. Jade closed her eyes and soon was in a dream. She was a captain of a boat; the sea was rough and pirates were chasing them. "What should we do, captain?" the crew asked Jade. "Sail ahead!" she heard herself saying. "To the ocean!"

The End